DreamWorks
DINOTRUX
ROLLING
WITH THE
ROLLODONS!

Adapted by Elizabeth Milton

LITTLE, BROWN & COMPANY

LB kids

Little, Brown and Company
Hachette Book Group
1290 Avenue of the Americas, New York, NY 10104
Visit us at lb-kids.com

First Edition: May 2017

LB kids is an imprint of Little, Brown and Company.
The LB kids name and logo are trademarks of Hachette Book Group, Inc.

The publisher is not responsible for websites (or their content) that are not owned by the publisher.

Library of Congress Control Number 2016946093

ISBNs: 978-0-316-43154-5 (paperback); 978-0-316-55363-6 (ebook); 978-0-316-55362-9 (ebook); 978-0-316-43156-9 (ebook)

Printed in the United States of America

CW

10 9 8 7 6 5 4 3 2 1

It started out as a peaceful day in the Crater. Ty and Revvit raced out of the Garage...and stopped in their tracks. Ty tried to inch forward, but nothing happened.

"Hey, I can't move!" he said. When he looked down, he saw sticky, black tar all over his treads.

"This is not good," said Revvit.

"Tell me about it," Dozer grumbled nearby. "I've been stuck here for hours!"

Skya was stuck, too. They had all rolled right into a tar pit!

After a deep clean, the Dinotrux were good as new. "I feel like a whole new Trux," Ty said as he exited the Trux Wash.

Dozer came out next. "I think you used up half the geyser in there," he teased.

Ty smiled sheepishly. "I had to wash behind my gears."

"I knew I forgot something," Dozer admitted.

Dozer wondered if D-Structs was to blame for all the tar.

Revvit didn't think so. "The tar seems to be coming up naturally on our most-traveled paths," he explained. "The ground is probably thinned from so much use."

"Trux *gotta* roll," Ty replied.

"Yes," Revvit said, "but we must find a way to keep the tar from seeping through the ground so we do not end up stuck living in a tar pit!"

Ty grabbed a mouthful of palm fronds and dropped them onto the bubbling black tar pit, being careful not to get too close. In seconds, the green fronds sank below the surface. Revvit realized that they needed to find something small enough to fill the cracks in the ground, and dense enough to keep the tar from oozing up again.

"We need rocks!" Revvit said.

"Then we need Ton-Ton," Ty replied, but Ton-Ton had left the Garage early that morning, and no one knew where he had gone. "Don't worry, I got it," Ty told Revvit. Then he used his wrecking-ball tail to break a big boulder into smaller rocks.

"Smaller pieces, Ty," Revvit directed. "Then, Dozer and Skya, spread them over the tar."

"Let's trux it up!" Ty shouted. He broke the rocks into smaller chunks, but when Dozer and Skya scattered them over the tar, the pieces were still too big to fill the cracks.

That's when they heard the unmistakable voice of Ton-Ton yelling, "Woo-hoo!"

A herd of steamrolling Trux was migrating, and Ton-Ton was rolling with them! "Hey, dudes, come on down! It's Rollodon season!" Ton-Ton yelled to his friends.

"Every year the Rollodons roll in, knock everything down, and then roll out," Dozer complained.

"It's the best time of year!" Ton-Ton shouted.

Ty noticed that the Rollodons did something else, too. "They flatten everything they roll over!" he told the Dinotrux. This gave Ty an idea...

If they could get the Rollodons to roll over the tar pit, their steamrollers might be able to crush the stones into pieces small enough to seal the cracks and keep the Crater from becoming a giant tar pit.

"That is a good plan, Ty, but it has just one flaw: the Rollodons! They are completely uncontrollable!" Revvit insisted.

But Ty wanted to give his plan a try. He caught up with the Rollodon herd and asked for their help with the tar pit, but they looked straight ahead and said, "Roll!" He asked them to turn toward the pit, and they said, "Roll!" All they *ever* said was a grumbly "Roll, roll, roll!"

Finally, Ty raced in front of the pack and roared as loudly as he could to get their attention. The Rollodons didn't stop rolling. They knocked him over!

"Ouch!" Ty said.

"Just one ouch?" Skya asked. "That looked like at least a two-oucher."

Skya tried next. She used her cable tongue like a lasso and roped it around a Rollodon's horn. "Yee-haw!" she yelled, but the Rollodon kept rolling... and pulled her along with him!

Dozer tried to corral the Rollodons. He dozed a wall to herd them toward the tar pit. It worked until the wall ended. The Rollodons kept rolling... right into Dozer!

"That's gonna dent," Ty said, cringing.

Ton-Ton said the Rollodons wouldn't roll into him because they had a deep connection. "I call it a brain-blend!" Ton-Ton boasted, but when he gave it a try, the Rollodons kept rolling...and tossed him from one Trux to the next. He finally landed upside down on a Rollodon near the back of the pack! "Hey! Dudes!" Ton-Ton said. "Not cool!"

The Rollodons wouldn't stop rolling no matter what the Trux did…and now they were heading straight toward Revvit and the Reptools at the Garage! This time, though, something surprising happened: The Rollodons swerved, and no one was hurt.

"If something hadn't spooked them, the Garage would be flattened," Waldo told the Dinotrux. "They just turned right before they hit Revvit."

Revvit was shaking. He was very scared of Rollodons. "This is not my first Rollodon rodeo," he confessed. "I was out exploring one day when I was a young tool, and got caught in a Rollodon run.

"They were charging right at me, but something spooked them. I barely escaped with my bits!"

"Revvit, did you ever think that whatever spooked them was—was you?" Ty asked. "Think about it. Both times they got close enough to see you, they veered away!"

Revvit couldn't believe it. Rollodons would trample a T-Trux, but if Ty was right, they were *afraid* of little Reptools! It gave Ty an idea for a plan, and Revvit caught on quickly. Rollodons might run toward the tar pit...to get away from Reptools!

"With correct placement of materials and strategic maneuvering of the Rollodons," Revvit said, chiseling a diagram onto a rock, "it could work."

The Dinotrux placed more stones and rocks that were ready to be crushed into the tar pit. Then they brought Ace, Waldo, Click-Clack, and Revvit to their positions... right in the path of the Rollodons!

Ace went first, and she kept things light when the Rollodons came toward her. "Howdy, boys! Happy to see me?" she asked.

"Roll!" said the Rollodons, but they moved out of Ace's way!

Then Waldo wrangled the Rollodons. "*Yah! Yah!* That-a way," he said, and they veered off toward Click-Clack.

Click-Clack closed his eyes and hung on to Skya's crane tongue as she lowered him to the ground. The Rollodons spotted him and changed direction.

Revvit was the next and last Reptool in line, and he was shaking with fear. He was still scared because of his first Rollodon run-in.

"We'll do this together, Rev," Ty offered.

"No, Ty, they may not even see me if we are together," Revvit said. "Besides, this is something I need to do for myself."

Ty set Revvit on the ground, and the Rollodons rolled toward him at top speed!

When the Rollodons got close enough to see Revvit, they changed course and rolled over the tar pit! Their steamrollers crushed the stones and sealed the cracks in the ground. Everyone in the Crater was finally safe! Ty and Revvit tail-bumped to celebrate, and the Rollodons continued on their migration, leaving behind a thin layer of tar that dried quickly into a smooth, paved surface made for rolling!

"What do you say we try out our new path?" Ty asked Skya, Dozer, and Ton-Ton.

The gleaming black pavement was so smooth on their treads that even Dozer glided around. "Gotta admit, this *is* pretty nice!" he said.

"Woo-hoo!" Ton-Ton cheered as he and Skya raced ahead. Rolling with the Dinotrux was even better than rolling with the Rollodons now, thanks to the Reptools!

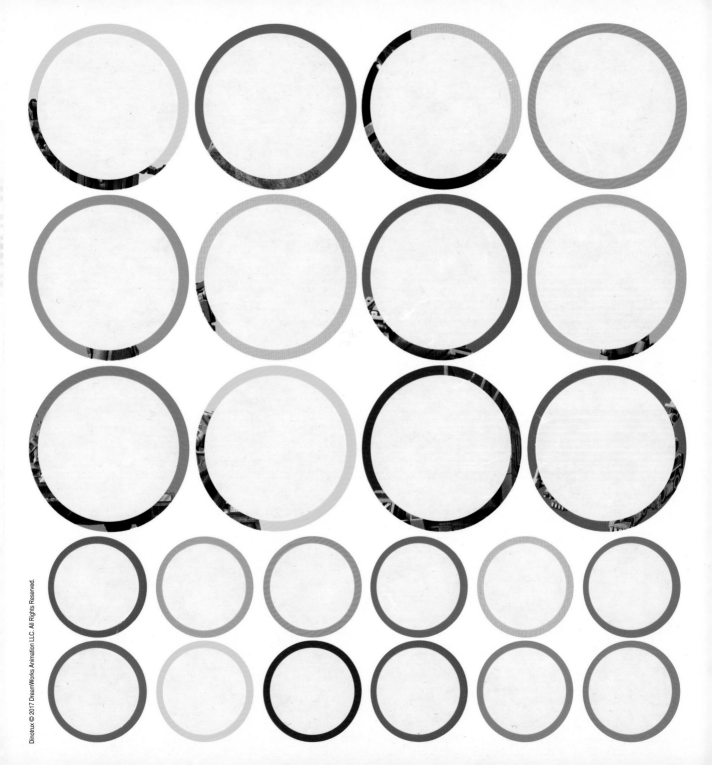